Tickly Octopus

For Roan, with love

ISBN-13: 978-0-545-01345-1
ISBN-10: 0-545-01345-3

Text and illustrations copyright © 2007 by Ruth Galloway.
All rights reserved. Published by Scholastic Inc., 557 Broadway, New York, NY 10012,
by arrangement with Tiger Tales, an imprint of ME Media, LLC. SCHOLASTIC and
associated logos are trademarks and/or registered trademarks of Scholastic Inc.

12 11 10 9 8 7 6 5 4 3 2 1   7 8 9 10 11 12/0

Printed in the U.S.A.   40

First Scholastic printing, May 2007

Tickly Octopus

by Ruth Galloway

SCHOLASTIC INC.
New York   Toronto   London   Auckland   Sydney
Mexico City   New Delhi   Hong Kong   Buenos Aires

Down in the ocean, among the swirling
seaweed and the colorful coral, lived
a tickly octopus.

He had eight twisty, twirly tentacles,
and he loved to use them to tickle.

When Octopus tickled the little fish they
jumped and jiggled and wiggled and giggled.
They thought tickling was tons of fun!

But most of the creatures found his tickling tiresome. Octopus tickled Starfish and made her squirm.

"Stop it!" she squeaked.

Octopus tickled clickety-clackety Crab, and Crab tripped and tumbled into the sand.

"Go away!" he snapped.

"But I'm a tickly octopus, and I'm really good at tickling," said Octopus sadly, and he swam off to tickle the wiggly, giggly fish again.

One day, Octopus saw Oyster snoozing among the seashells. He couldn't resist giving her one teeny tiny tickle.

But Oyster woke with a jump and
dropped her precious pearl.

PING! BIP! BOING! It bounced over the
rocks and was swept away by the current.

"Oh no!" gasped Octopus.

Poor Oyster was very upset.

"Sorry!" said Octopus. "I'll get it back for you."

Octopus raced through the water with a WHOOSH and a SWOOSH! "Wheee!" he thought. "I never knew I could be so super speedy."

Octopus followed the pearl as it
tumbled to the bottom of the sea.
"Wow!" he thought. "I never knew
I could swim so deep!"

At last, Octopus reached
the pearl, but...
PLINK!
PLONK!
PLOP!

Oyster's precious pearl
bounced over the rocks and
slipped through a small gap
in the ocean floor.

Octopus squished and squashed and heaved and squeezed...

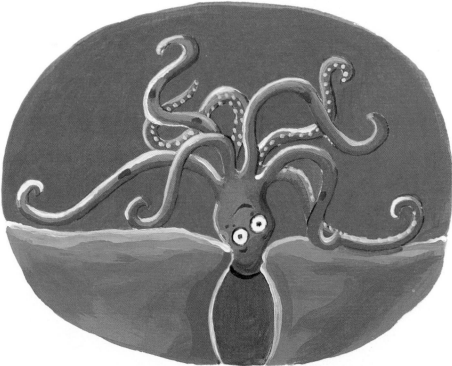

and managed to push his rubbery body through the gap.

"Ooh!" he thought. "I never knew I could be so slinky!"

There, glinting in the darkness,
was the smooth and shiny pearl.
But just behind it was a fierce eel!

"Yikes!" squeaked Octopus.
He quickly picked up the pearl
and sped away.

"GIVE ME THAT PEARL!"
roared the eel.

Octopus huffed and puffed as the eel chased him. He'd swum such a long way and he was very tired. The eel was getting closer and closer....

With a spurt and a squirt, a belch and a squelch, Octopus sprayed a cloud of black ink. The eel couldn't see a thing!

"Oh, my!" thought Octopus.
"I never knew I could be so
inky." And he danced happily
back to Oyster.

Oyster was delighted to get her pearl back.

"I promise I won't ever tickle you again," Octopus said. "I've found lots of other things I'm good at doing. From now on I'm going to be a...

speedy,

deep-sea,

slinky,

inky octopus...

"but I'll still be a little tickly, too!"